בס"ד
לד' הארץ ומלואה

**This book belongs to:**

Please read it to me!

## My Sometimes Feelings

For my sister Valerie... and all the feelings we share. – L.R.

To our precious grandchildren...we feel blessed. – A. J. W

First Edition - Adar 5778 / March 2018

Editor: D. L. Rosenfeld
Managing Editor: Yossi Leverton
Layout: Moshe Cohen

ISBN:  978-1-945560-07-1
LCCN:  2017961061

**HACHAI PUBLISHING**
Brooklyn, New York
Tel: 718-633-0100  Fax: 718-633-0103
www.hachai.com   info@hachai.com

Printed in China

GLOSSARY

Shabbos.....................Sabbath

Hashem......................G-d

Mitzvos.......................Commandments; Good deeds

# My Sometimes Feelings

by Leah Rubabshi, MSW
illustrated by Amy Wummer

Hachai
PUBLISHING

**H**ashem made me special, as special can be,
There's no one who feels just exactly like me.

Sometimes I feel

# happy

I'm laughing out loud!
My smile is the biggest
You'll see in a crowd.

Sometimes I feel

## sad

And I just don't know why.
It helps me feel better
To have a good cry.

Sometimes I feel

# angry

I'm ready to shout!

I take some
deep breaths

Till that feeling fades out.

Sometimes I feel

**calm**

And relaxed when I rest.
Especially on Shabbos,
The day I like best.

Sometimes I'm

# excited

I'm bouncing around.
It's hard to keep both
Of my feet on the ground!

Sometimes I feel

# bored

Because nothing is new.

But somehow, I always find something to do.

Sometimes I feel

# brave

I feel mighty and strong!
I hold my head high
When new things come along.

Sometimes I feel

**scared**

I have worries and fears.

I think of Hashem,
Then the fear disappears.

Sometimes I feel
# silly
And act like a clown.

I make
funny faces

And jump
up and down!

Sometimes I feel

**shy**

When I meet someone new.
It helps me feel better
If they feel shy too.

Sometimes I feel

# sorry

For words that I said.

I ask for forgiveness
And feel good instead.

Sometimes I feel
# loving
And caring and kind.

I look for
more mitzvos,

The most I can find!

With all of these

# feelings

That live inside me,
I don't always know what my feelings will be.

Some feelings will change,
And some might go away.
Do you know the feelings you're feeling today?

## NOTE TO PARENTS AND TEACHERS:

In Jewish thought, a truly strong person is one who has
mastered his own emotions and conquered his own desires.
Teaching young children to identify and name their feelings is
the first step on a lifelong journey toward emotional health
and spiritual growth.

Learning to identify and express all types of feelings plants
the seeds for strong coping skills later in life. Rather than
dismissing sadness with a reflexive "Don't cry," it's important
to convey that all feelings have value. Sadness can fuel empathy.
Boredom can lead to action.

Children who are encouraged to express anger with words and not
hands, are well on their way to establishing genuine relationships,
effective communication, self control, and a positive self image.

Certainly, when adults take the time to acknowledge all kinds
of emotions, it helps children feel loved, understood, and
deeply connected to their caregivers.

For use at home or in the classroom, a feelings chart
includes even more options to help children identify
and name exactly what they feel.